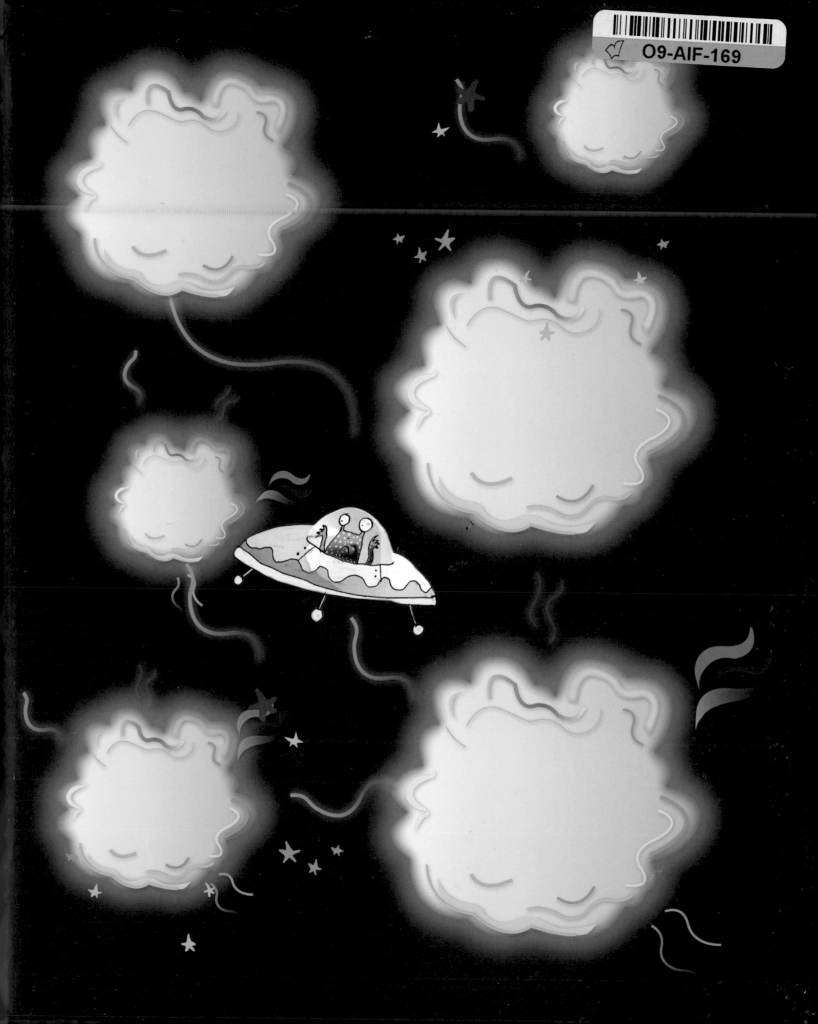

This book belongs to:

....

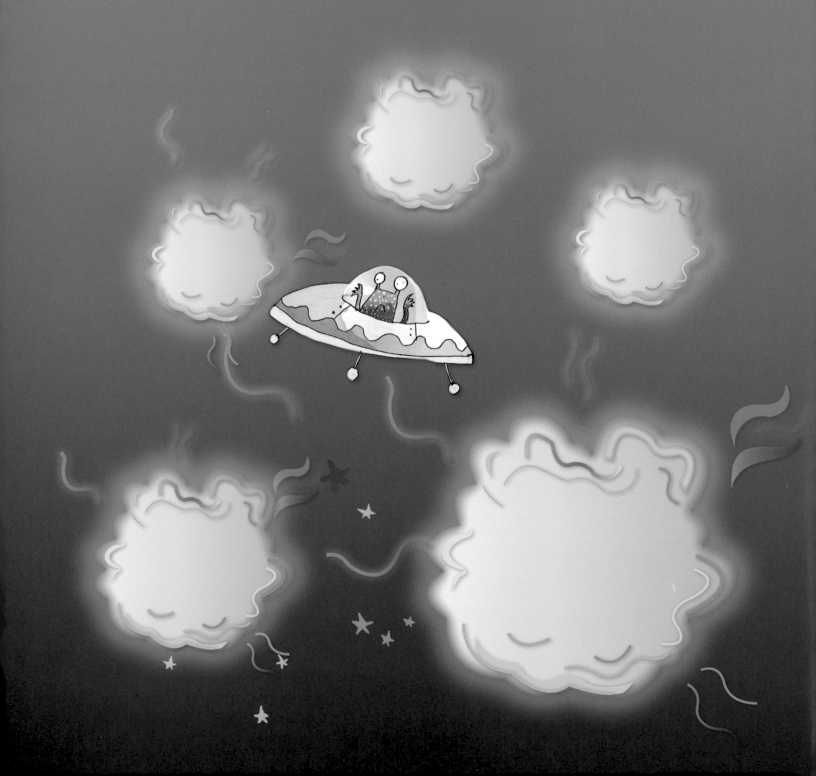

The Super Smelly ALIEN!

Written by
Ricky Lauder

A SCRATCH-
AND-SNIFF BOOK

PSS!

Down on Moldy Moon, in a valley made of cheese,
Alvin was playing with his jimpy-jumpy fleas.

"Come on," he said. "I'm bored of this place!"
So Alvin and his fleas zoomed off into space.

Whizzing past the stars in his supersonic ship,
Cluster Crater was the first stop of his exciting trip.

But the fleas hopped all over the Big-Footed Boos.
"Ugh, gross!" they cried. "We're not playing with you!"

At Lunar Lake, Alvin's landing went awry.
The ship hit the middle of a cosmic cow pie!

The One-Eyed Woggles were covered, head to toe.
"Oh dear," said the fleas, "we really need to go!"

There was a yummy picnic at their next exciting stop.
One alien asked Alvin, "Would you like some galactic pop?"

With a curly, whirly straw, Alvin took a big slurp.
But suddenly he let out the most enormous BURP!

Down a black hole they whizzed and whirled.
"Wheee!" said the fleas, as they swirled and twirled.

"Don't stop here!" said the Piggles with a scowl.
"The smell from your ship is simply foul!"

"Mmm," said Alvin. "I can smell something yummy.
Let's land at Crunchy Comet and eat something scrummy."

But too many treats made his big tummy grumble.
Then his bottom did a toot that made the ground rumble!

Bursting with pretty perfumes galore,
the next place made Alvin feel worse than before.

The Pufflings covered him in sweet-smelling sprays.
Running off he cried, "I won't smell stinky for days!"

Twisting and turning, they landed safely on the ground.
In Twilight Town, stardust was falling all around.

The dust made Alvin's nose tickle. Suddenly he went, "Achoo!"
He covered the Long-Nosed Noodles in green galactic goo!

At Cosmic Creek, the Fibbles were playing in the sun.
"Can I join in, too?" said Alvin. "We'll have lots of fun."

"Let's play," he said, throwing stinky space pies.
"We don't like smelly stuff, Alvin!" the aliens cried.

At Meteor Meadow, the Polettes held their little noses,
as Alvin's super stench killed their daisies and roses.

The aliens shouted, "Take your fleas and go away!
You smell gross. We don't want to play today."

Alvin and his fleas were far from home.
They had made no friends and were all alone.

With tears in his eyes, Alvin took a big sniff,
when he smelled the most delicious whiff!

"This is Planet Stink," the Stinky Snoggles said with glee.
"We'll play with you and your jimpy-jumpy fleas!"

With lots of gross smells, stink, goo, and slime,
Alvin and his fleas had the most wonderful time!

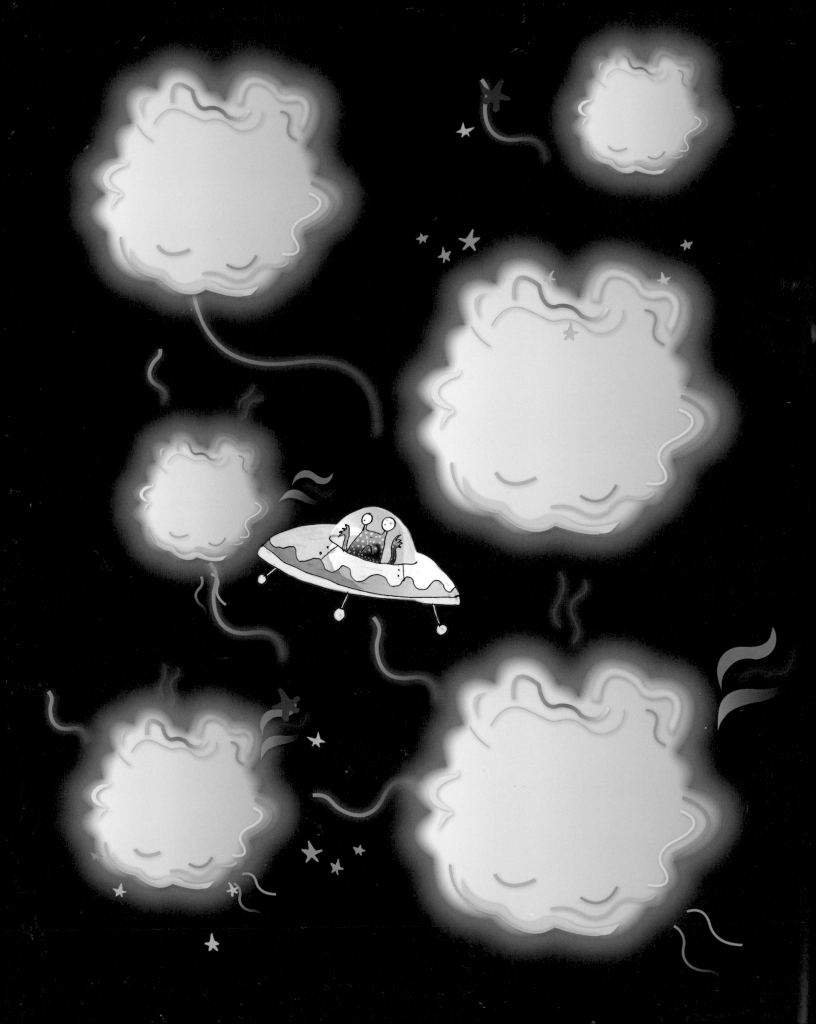